Whales

WRITTEN & PHOTOGRAPHED
BY KIM WESTERSKOV, Ph.D.

Dominie Press, Inc.

A southern right whale up close. These whales are gentle giants: slow swimming, curious, and generally calm.

1

Introducing Whales

I have watched sei whales and Bryde's (pronounced "broo-dahs") whales swimming around our yacht. During trips to **Antarctica**, minke whales followed our **icebreaker** as it cut a path through the sea ice toward the coast. Killer whales were there, too, diving under the broken ice and patrolling along the ice edge, ever on the lookout for a meal of **penguins** or seals.

Each of those times was wonderful.

NOTES

Many years ago I had a dream. I wanted to photograph and swim with some of the largest animals ever to have lived on earth—the large whales. Blue whales are still on my "one day, perhaps..." list, but over the past fifteen years I have swum with humpback whales, right whales, sperm whales, minke whales, pilot whales, and killer whales.

▲ *A calf at its mother's side.*

Perhaps the most magical were the times when a curious baby whale left its mother's side to swim over and take a close look at me. One young whale swam so close that I could have touched it. And on another occasion, a baby whale picked me up with its flipper and carried me along while it looked me over. Our eyes were only two feet apart. I have no idea what a baby whale remembers, but I will never forget that wonderful moment.

2

What Is a Whale?

▲ *Whales need to breathe air, like all mammals, though they can hold their breath for a long time.*

Whales are **mammals**, like humans. But they are sea mammals that never need to come ashore. They are warm-blooded and breathe air. The mothers give birth to live young, which they feed with their own milk. They are good swimmers, though not all whales move fast in the water. Whales often cruise slowly when they're not in a hurry, but some can reach speeds of thirty-five miles an hour. Fastest among the whales are orcas and the large rorquals: sei, fin, and blue whales.

▲ *This is the "blow," or "spout," of a minke whale.*

Most fish swim by moving their tails and bodies from side to side, but whales swim by moving their powerful **tail flukes** up and down. They use their flippers for balance and steering. Whales breathe through a single blowhole or double blowhole located in the top of the head. The blowholes close tightly when the whales are underwater. Experts can often identify a type of whale just from the size and shape of its "blow," or "spout."

Whales have a layer of fat under their skin called blubber that is nearly two feet thick in some whales. Blubber is used as a means of controlling their temperature and storing food, so that they can go for many months without eating. It can act like a wetsuit, keeping the whales warm; but it also can be used for cooling them down.

▾ *The powerful tail fluke of a right whale, as seen up close.*

Two Types of Whales

There are two types of whales:

Toothed whales have teeth to catch and hold their **prey**. There are about seventy **species** of toothed whales, including sperm whales, all dolphins and porpoises, and some small whales: beaked whales, narwhal, and belugas.

Baleen whales have rows of baleen, or "whalebone," hanging from the roof of their mouth, much like the teeth of a huge comb. The baleen acts like a sieve, or strainer, that traps small animals in the whale's mouth. Baleen is made of keratin, the same material as your hair and fingernails. The eleven species of baleen whales include all of the big whales, except sperm whales.

The powerful tail fluke of a sperm whale, the largest of the toothed whales.

Dolphins are actually small toothed whales.

This is a humpback whale, one of the baleen whales.

Baleen whales are divided into two main groups: four species of right whales, and six species of rorquals: blue, fin, sei, Bryde's, minke, and humpback whales.

4

Where Whales Live

Some whales, such as orcas and minke whales, are found in all seas, from tropical waters to polar ice. Other whales are found only in certain areas. For example, bowhead whales live at the edge of the Arctic pack ice, and Bryde's whales live only in warm seas. Some orca populations stay in more or less the same place, while others travel large distances.

Right whales and gray whales are often seen in shallow water close to shore, so we know quite a lot about them. But the twenty-one or more

The minke whale is found in all seas, from the tropics to the pack ice of the polar seas.

The Bryde's whale lives only in warm seas, and is sometimes called the tropical whale. It is the only baleen whale that does not migrate to cold-water feeding areas in summer. ▸

species of beaked whales live in deep water far from land, and we know very little about them. In fact, some of them are known only from a few skulls. A new species of beaked whale has just been discovered, and more species could yet be found.

Most baleen whales spend their summers in cold, plankton-rich seas around Antarctica and in **Arctic seas**. There they feed, building up large stores of blubber that will last them through a winter in **tropical seas**, where there is little or no food. While traveling and at their breeding grounds, adult whales usually do not eat; instead, they use up the food reserves stored in their blubber. Baleen whales spend nearly as much time in **migration** as they do at their feeding and breeding grounds.

5

What They Eat

Toothed whales are hunters. They **prey** on squid and fish, which they catch one at a time. Their sharp teeth are designed to catch and hold slippery creatures, which are swallowed whole rather than chewed.

A baleen whale takes in huge mouthfuls of water containing its prey, usually **krill** or small fish. It then closes its mouth and uses its tongue to squirt the water out through the baleen. The stiff hairs of the baleen form a strainer that traps the prey. Then the whale licks the food off its baleen and swallows it.

◂ *An orca carries around a stingray before eating it.*

These minke whales are coming up for breath between feeding dives in food-rich Antarctic seas. ▸

▲ *The long grooves on the throat of rorqual whales, such as this humpback whale, allow them to gulp huge mouthfuls of water. Their prey is caught as the whale forces out the water through its baleen.*

The baleen whale catches its prey in two ways. The right whale is a "strainer." It simply swims along with its huge mouth open, feeding as it goes. The rorqual is more of a "gulper." It has long grooves on its throat and chest, which expand like the bellows of an accordion, allowing the whale to open its mouth very wide. A rorqual usually lunges into large schools of krill or fish, and gulps a huge mouthful of water and food. The grooves stretch, and the whale's throat bulges out like a huge balloon. A blue whale can hold seventy tons of water in one mouthful! As the giant mouth closes, the tongue forces the water out through the baleen filters.

6

The Circle of Life

How long do whales live? Probably about as long as humans, and within just as wide a range. Some humans live to be 120 years old, but many don't even reach forty. Small whales may live for up to fifty years; large ones can live twice as long.

Some whales live more than a century! Bowhead whales in Alaska easily reach 150 years of age, and one was estimated to have been 211 years old when it was harpooned by hunters.

Humpback whales are among the most energetic whales, especially at their breeding grounds. ▸

▲ *Orca teeth marks are visible on this sperm whale's tail fluke. Even the largest whales are not safe from orcas.*

Whales normally have only one **calf** at a time. Birth takes place underwater, and it may take a few hours. The mother or another female often helps the calf to the surface, where it takes its first breath. The calf is protected and nursed for about a year. The mother's rich milk is pumped into the calf's mouth. Fathers take no part in caring for the young.

Whales have few enemies. Large sharks and orcas are their **predators**. So are humans. Whales are still killed by whalers from a few countries. Whales also die from disease, **parasites**, injuries, and strandings. Some are hit by ships, accidentally trapped in fishing nets, and weakened or killed by **pollution**.

7

Whales, Large and Small

The heaviest animal ever to have lived on Earth is the blue whale. Some of the biggest dinosaurs—with their long necks and tails—may have been longer, but none were as heavy. The blue whale can weigh up to 190 tons, though most adults weigh up to 120 tons. A single blue whale can eat up to eight tons of food in one day.

▲ *Killer whales, or orcas, are the largest members of the dolphin family.*

What is the smallest whale? The words *whale*, *dolphin*, and *porpoise* cause some confusion. They are all in a group of mammals

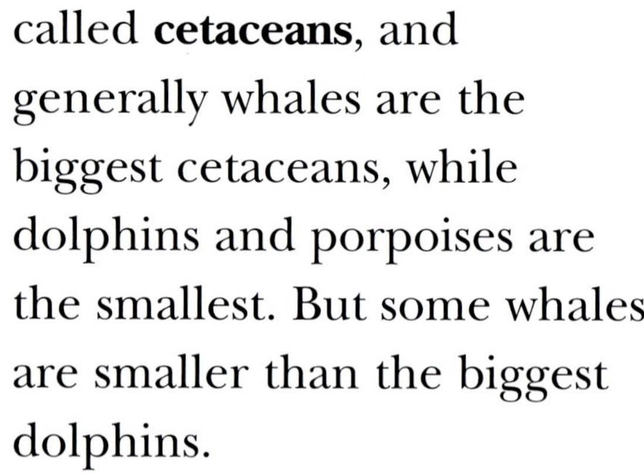

Right whale mother and calf

called **cetaceans**, and generally whales are the biggest cetaceans, while dolphins and porpoises are the smallest. But some whales are smaller than the biggest dolphins.

The pygmy killer whale is one of six whales, including killer whales and pilot whales, that are actually large dolphins. Even more confusing, these six species are often called blackfish, even though not all of them are black—and they are mammals, not fish. The smallest "true whale" is the dwarf sperm whale, which grows to a length of nine feet.

▲ *These three young right whales are just "hanging around" on the winter breeding grounds.*

Right Whales

The right whale is one of the biggest whales, and one of the heaviest animals ever to live on Earth. Although not as long as the fin whale, it can reach the same weight, about 100 tons. Up to sixty-five feet long, it is a gentle, often playful whale. It is easy to recognize because its wide back has no fin.

Right whales often breach, launching themselves into the air, headfirst, and falling back into the water with a huge splash.

Right whales were so named by hunters because they were the "right" whales to hunt. They were easy to catch, being slow swimmers. And they are often found close to shore. In addition, they float when they are dead, whereas many other types of whales sink when they die. And the right whale was a rich source of oil and whalebone.

Right whales were hunted nearly to extinction by 1850. In the **northern hemisphere**, they have not recovered and still hover close to extinction, with a population of about 300 animals. In the **southern hemisphere**, there has been a slow recovery in recent years, and there are now about 8,000 southern right whales.

Sperm Whales

The world's largest toothed predator is the sperm whale. Bull sperm whales are usually about sixty feet long and weigh up to sixty tons. Females are much smaller, usually about forty feet long. The largest meat-eating dinosaurs grew to about forty feet in length and weighed up to eight tons.

Sperm whales are found in all oceans, usually offshore in deep water. They are seen close to shore only where there is deep water near the coast. ▸

▲ *A sperm whale arches its back as it gets ready to dive. With its tail fluke raised high in the air, the whale now begins its dive toward the seafloor far below.*

The sperm whale is an amazing creature. It has the largest brain of any animal on earth, and it can dive as deep as two miles. During these deep dives, a sperm whale holds its breath for up to two hours—or more!

The main part of the sperm whale's **diet** is squid. We know that sperm whales occasionally catch giant squid, which grow to nearly forty feet in length, but most of the squid they catch are less than three feet long.

How do sperm whales catch fast-moving squid in the total darkness of the deep ocean? We don't know for sure, but some scientists think that sperm whales stun their prey with bursts of loud sound—a kind of underwater stun gun!

A sperm whale begins a dive. ▶

10

Humpback Whales

Humpbacks are one of the best-known whales, and they are often the favorites on whale-watching trips. They show little fear of boats and are often curious. They are big whales, usually about fifty feet long, and they can weigh up to forty tons.

Their stout bodies are not **streamlined**, but humpbacks are energetic, graceful swimmers underwater. Their breaches are spectacular and often repeated many times. One humpback whale was seen breaching over 200 times—one breach after another.

The tall blow of a humpback whale, here migrating along a coastline on its way from its summer feeding grounds in Antarctica to its winter breeding grounds in the tropics. ▸

Humpback whales are "singing whales." Males sing beautiful songs, the longest and most complex songs in the animal kingdom. Each song lasts up to half an hour and can be repeated for hours. These songs can be heard underwater over twenty miles away.

Humpbacks have many ways of catching their food. The most impressive of these is "bubble-netting," where the whales swim in big circles under schools of fish. As they swim, the whales blow air from their blowholes, forming a "net" of noisy bubbles that surrounds the fish, driving them into the center of the "net." The whales then swim up through the center and swallow the water that holds the most fish.

▲ *This baby humpback whale already weighs about two tons.*

◀ *A humpback whale takes a dive.*

11

Whales and People

Whales have little reason to be grateful to human beings. Over the centuries, people have killed millions of whales, each one a painful death. No whale has yet become **extinct**, but some species are in serious trouble. And yet whalers from a few countries, particularly Japan and Norway, still hunt and kill them.

In addition to whalers, pollution is a serious threat to whales. Pollutants of many kinds are dumped into the sea each day: poisons, fertilizers, pesticides, sewage, plastics, and many more. Add oil spills to this **toxic** mix,

Here, a diver experiences a close encounter with a curious, gentle giant.

▲ *Tourists enjoy whale watching at Kaikoura, New Zealand.*

NOTES

Not only does whale watching employ people, it also changes people. I have seen people suddenly transformed when they meet whales or dolphins up close. Then they realize what wonderful animals these creatures are—and that we must do all we can to protect them. The future of whales depends mostly on you and me—all of us.

and you can understand why whales are weakened and killed by pollution. Whales also become tangled in fishing nets or are accidentally rammed by large ships. People also over-fish the oceans, robbing whales of their food supply.

Fortunately, attitudes are changing. Today, many people

are working hard to save whales and protect the seas in which they live. The best hope for whales might lie in whale watching, when people reach for a camera instead of a harpoon. Every year over 10 million people in nearly 100 countries go whale watching, making it one of the world's fastest-growing tourist activities.

▾ *The crew from an icebreaker in Antarctica watches a minke whale in open water behind the ship.*

Glossary

Antarctica: An uninhabited continent surrounding the South Pole

Arctic Seas: Waters surrounding the cold, barren region near the North Pole

Calf: A young animal

Cetaceans: Large aquatic mammals that have a streamlined body; a group of mammals made up of dolphins, porpoises, and whales

Diet: The food that an animal or a person usually eats

Extinct: To gradually disappear due to diminishing numbers

Icebreaker: A ship with a reinforced bow used to cut through thick ice and create a passage through frozen seas

Krill: A very small shrimp-like marine animal that is a primary source of food for penguins, whales, and many other inhabitants of Antarctica

Mammals: A class of warm-blooded animals in which the female feeds the young with its own milk

Migration: The movement of large numbers of animals from one region or habitat to another in response to cyclical seasonal changes

Northern Hemisphere: The half of the Earth located north of the equator

Parasites: Plants or animals that live on or in other, larger plants or animals and draw their nourishment from them

Penguins: Flightless, web-footed seabirds that use their flipper-shaped wings for swimming

Pollution: Contamination

Predators: Animals that hunt, catch, and eat other animals

Prey (n): Animals that are hunted and eaten by other animals

Prey (v): To stalk, or hunt, an animal or group of animals

Southern Hemisphere: The half of the Earth located south of the equator

Species: Types of animals that have some physical characteristics in common

Streamlined: Designed to move very quickly and gracefully

Tail Flukes: The part of a whale or dolphin's tail used to propel the animal through the water

Toxic: Poisonous; destructive or very harmful

Tropical Seas: Bodies of water that are very warm throughout the year